It was a beautiful day in the neighborhood, and Daniel was playing jungle with Tigey before bed.

Daniel asked Dad Tiger to play along too. "You are the best at playing jungle!" Daniel said.

But Dad couldn't play. "Sorry, my fuzzy guy," Dad said. "Remember, Mom and I are going out. Look who's here to take care of you!"

"Prince Tuesday! I'm getting a babysitter tonight!" Daniel said with excitement.

Prince Tuesday said, "I will take rrroyally good care of you until your parents come back home."

But Daniel didn't want Mom and Dad to leave. Daniel felt sad and said, "I'm going to miss you."

Mom said, "We will miss you too, but we'll come back at the end of the night."

Then Mom and Dad sang, *"Grown-ups come back."*

Dad said, "And when we get back home and you're asleep, we'll give you a kiss."

Daniel smiled, and he sang, *"Grown-ups come back."*

After Mom and Dad left, Daniel asked, "But now who's going to play jungle with me?"

"Your babysitter can!" said Prince Tuesday. "Watch out for that snake!" He jumped into the cave, and Daniel followed.

Daniel's babysitter was fun to play jungle with, just like Dad Tiger.

It was almost Daniel's bedtime. Prince Tuesday said, "Let's go through the jungle to get to your room!"

Mom Tiger and Dad Tiger usually help Daniel get ready for bed. Daniel asked, "Who will help me pick out my pajamas?"

"Your babysitter can!" said Prince Tuesday. Daniel's babysitter helped pick out his favorite Trolley pajamas, just like Mom and Dad.

Daniel went to the potty and brushed his teeth. "But who's going to tuck me into bed and read me a story?" Daniel asked.

"Your babysitter can!" said Prince Tuesday. Daniel chose a book and hopped into bed. Prince Tuesday read with silly voices, just like Mom and Dad!

Daniel was all ready for bed, except . . . he couldn't find Tigey! "Mom and Dad always know where Tigey is," said Daniel. "Now who will help me find Tigey?"

"Your babysitter can!" said Prince Tuesday. They looked all around the house.

"Do you see Tigey?" asked Daniel. He was worried.

They looked some more and soon found
Tigey! Daniel got back into bed.

But he still missed Mom and Dad. So Prince Tuesday sang, *"Grown-ups come back."*

Prince Tuesday was a grr-ific babysitter. Finally, Daniel went to sleep.

Mom and Dad came home, just like they said they would. They quietly sang, "*Grown-ups come back.* Goodnight, Daniel. Goodnight, Tigey. Ugga Mugga!"